STICK AND STONE

EXPLORE AND MORE

BETH FERRY
KRISTEN CELLA

CLARION BOOKS
Imprints of HarperCollinsPublishers

CONTENTS

STICK AND STONE

AND THE NATURE GIRL

Stone, want to help me with the peas?
Are the bees still there?
Yes, but they won't hurt you.
They scare me.
But you're a stone.
What could they do to you?

Are you afraid of monsters?

Um, I guess so.

Well, if you can be afraid of monsters,
I can be afraid of bees.

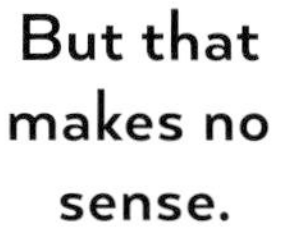
But that makes no sense.
There aren't any monsters around.

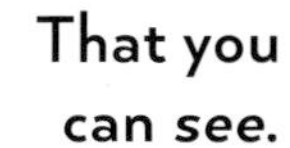
That you can see.

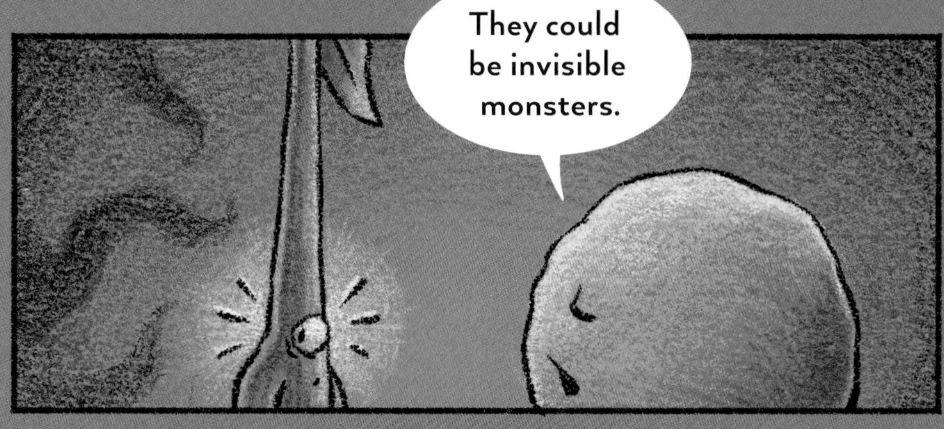
They could be invisible monsters.

Hmm,
I guess you're
right.
You can
stay afraid of
bees.
Thank you.
Stone?
Are *you*
afraid of
monsters?
There's
no such
thing as
monsters,
silly.

Stone, there's a Nature Girl in the forest.
What's a Nature Girl?
I don't know, but she's snooping around.
Let's go see.

Should we be afraid of her, too?

I don't know.

Look! There she is!

Here I am with my net,
scooping up the alphabet.
Nature Girls can look and see
awesome things from A to Z.

I spy with my little eye . . .
a girl.
And the sun.
And a butterfly.
The rare and elusive golden butterfly?

No. Just a plain white one.
Oh, bummer. But, Stone, we're not playing I Spy.
We're spying on the girl. Focus!

I am. I am focusing my eye on the Nature Girl!
Good!

M is for . . .

. . . *moss.*

Moss is
so soft.
I'd like to wrap
it around me
like a blanket.
I'd wrap
myself
up in a
spider's
web.

Yuck!
Too sticky.

Sticky for
Stick.
You're silly
today, Stone.

N is for . . . hmm.
What starts with N?
Nature starts with N,
but I can't put nature in my bucket.

Oh, look—
she found N.
Perfect!

Oh, oh, what starts with O?

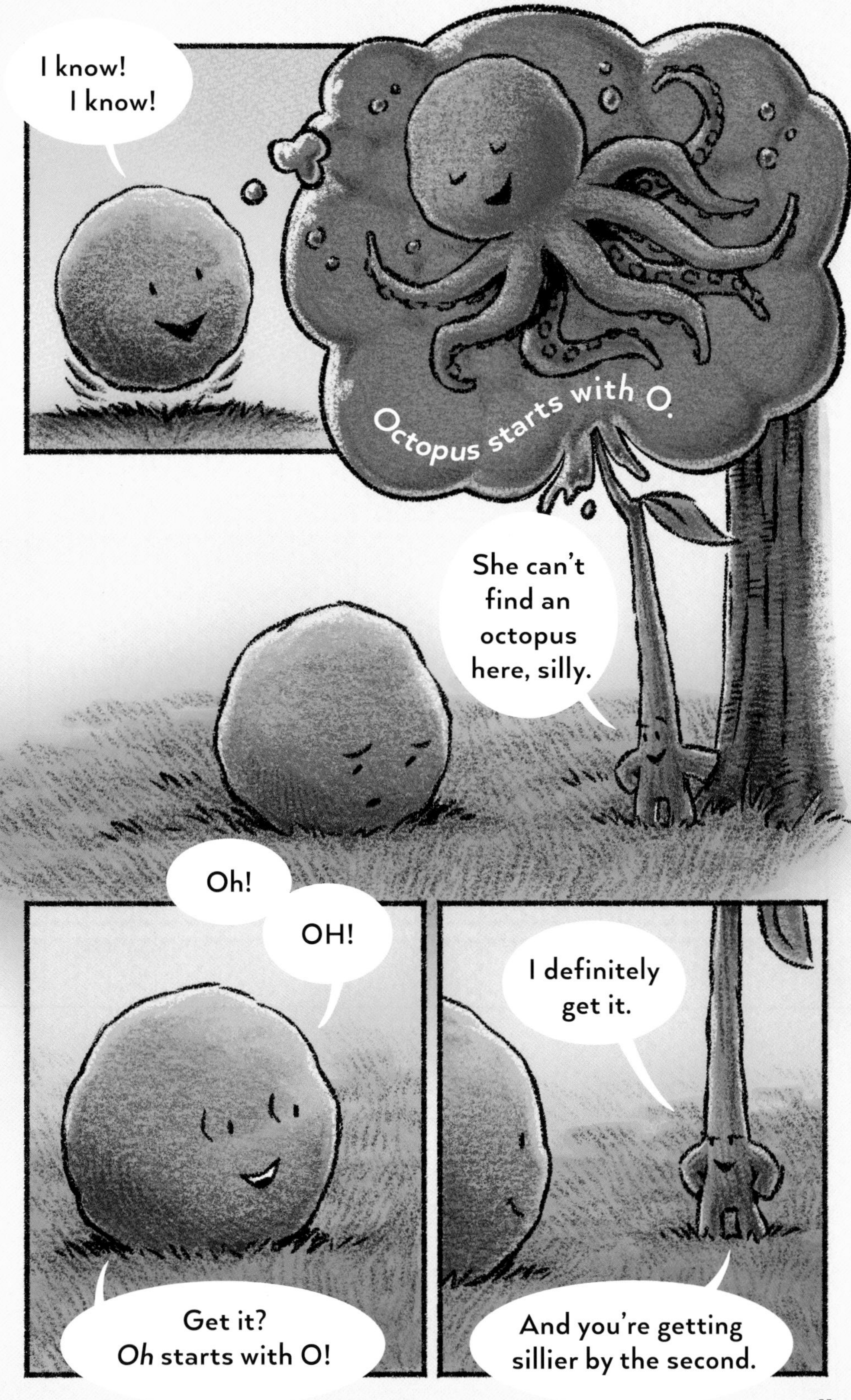
I know!
I know!
Octopus starts with O.
She can't find an octopus here, silly.
Oh!
OH!
Get it?
Oh starts with O!
I definitely get it.
And you're getting sillier by the second.

Oak leaf! Yes!

L, M, N, O, P.

Stick! This is our favorite song!

Q,
R,
S,
T,
U,
V...

P...P...
What starts with P?

OH NO

What?
What?

There's Pinecone.
Pinecone starts with P.

So does *peapod*.
Maybe she'll pick your peapods.
Not my peapods! They're so little.

But that's better than Pinecone, right?
Right?

Oh my!
Run, Pinecone,
run!
It's too late.
There . . .
goes . . .
Pinecone!
HELP!
You'll be okay,
Pinecone.
She seems really
nice.
Easy for
you to
saaaaaaaay.

Q, R, S,
T, U, V,
W,
X,
Y,
and Z.
Stone! Stop singing.
She just scooped up Pinecone.
Think about what's coming next!
Q.
After that.
R?
No, after that! S is coming.

Well, that's easy.
Stone starts with S.

So does *Stick*!

Oh,
I see.

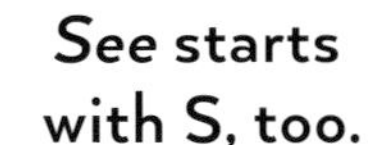
See starts with S, too.

Focus,
Stone!

She is only
going to pick
one S.

What are we
going to do?
I don't know!

Wait.
Wait.

She'll never
find a Q.
It'll be
okay.

Q, Q, what
to do?

Wait!
Is that a . . . ?

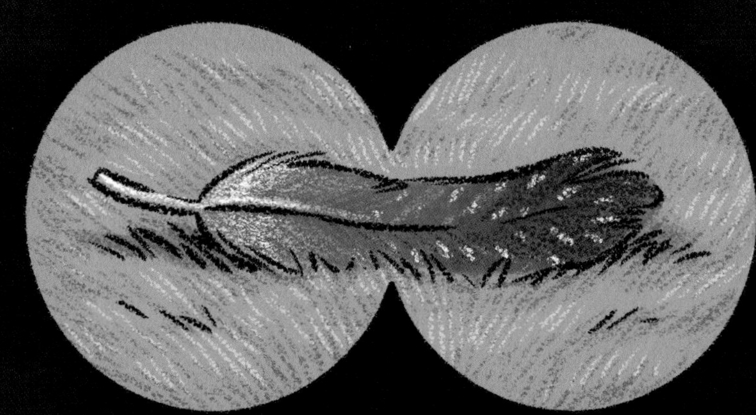

It's a *quail feather*!
Quail

Sweet!
Sweet!

It is *not* sweet.
It is sour. Definitely sour.
Sweet and *sour* both start with S.
I like this alphabet business!

What's going to happen?

Who's she going to pick?

I can't take the stress!

Rock for R.

Rock? *Rock*?
I'm not a rock.

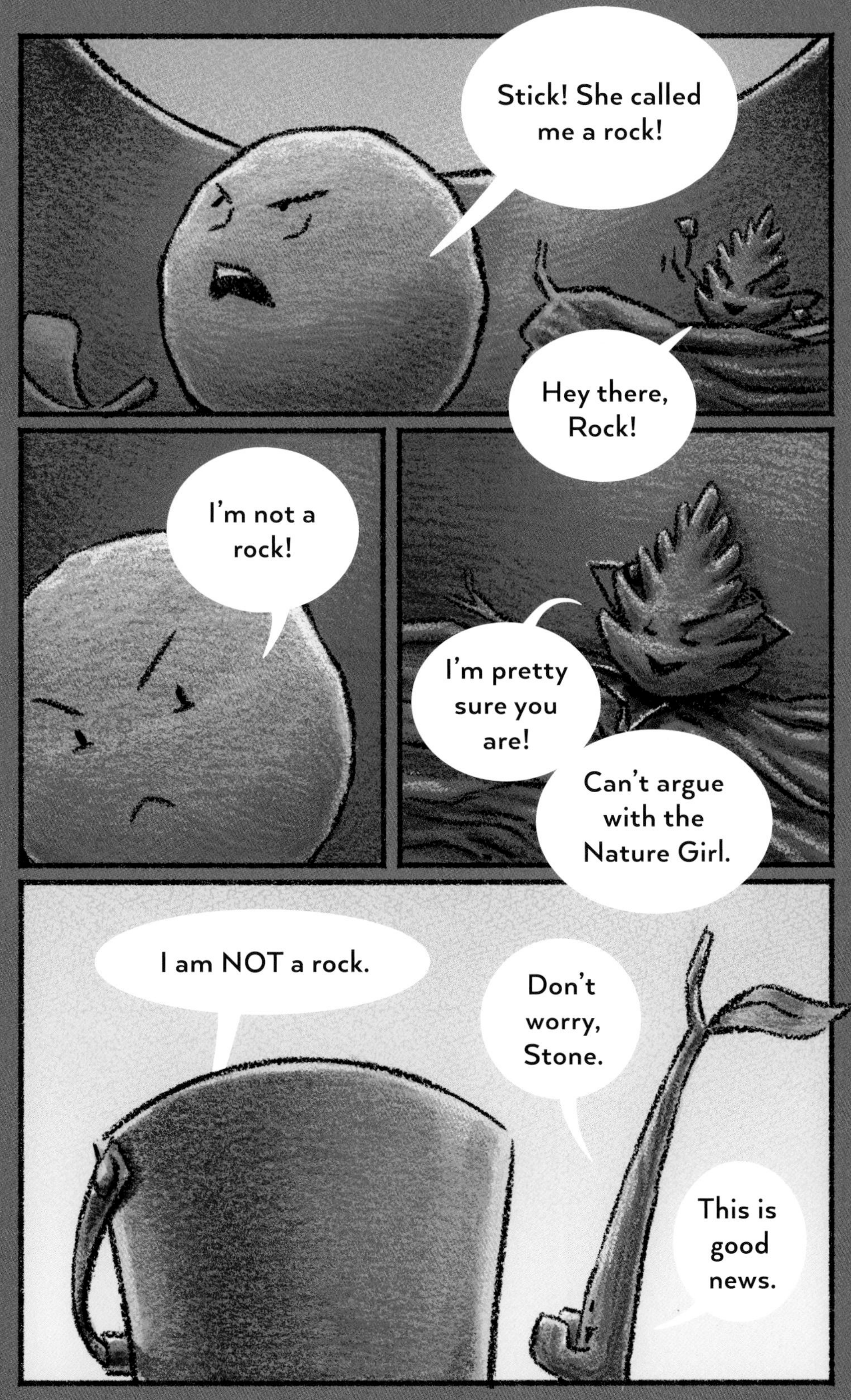
Stick! She called me a rock!
Hey there, Rock!
I'm not a rock!
I'm pretty sure you are!
Can't argue with the Nature Girl.
I am NOT a rock.
Don't worry, Stone.
This is good news.

She'll pick me for S and then we'll be back together.
I hope you're right.
It's hot in here.
Don't worry. She sees me. She'll be picking me up any second.
Any second.
Any . . .

Oh, look.
Double S.

A *snail shell*!

NOOOOOO

Stiiiiick!

A B C D E F G H I J K L M N O P Q R

Oh, woe is me!

Oh, woe is you!

Oh, woe is us!

T . . .

T . . .

What starts with T?

Twig!

Twig?
Twig?
She thinks I'm a twig?
Hey, Twig.

I'm not a twig.
Are you sure about that?
This Nature Girl knows her stuff.
At least we're together.
Hi!
Hi!
Do you know what's happening?

Not really, but she has a nice voice.

Do you know where we're going?

No, but I made some new friends. Say hi to Beetle and Corn.

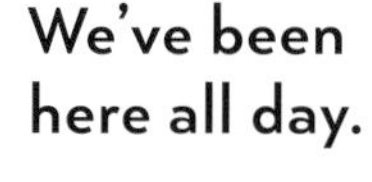
We've been here all day.

I'm so hot, I could pop!

ROAR!
ROAR!!

Why is that flower roaring at us?

Shhh. Don't look at her.

Don't talk to her.

I'm just trying to be brave.

It's scary in here.

I roar.

I cover myself with leaves!

I like to sing.

This Nature Girl's got to be done soon.

Just be brave a little longer.

What letter is she up to?

Zoo?
Zoos aren't part of nature!
Zero?
How do you put zero in a net?
Do you have rocks in your head?
Well, at least I'm trying!
What do *you* think it could be?
A *zebra*?

A zebra!
Where is she going to find a zebra?

I know! In Africa!

But we're not in Africa. We're in the forest.

Are there forests in Africa?

Well, I don't know.
All I know is this Rock is sitting on my head.

I'm Stone!

Don't let him bother you, Stone.
Wait! Wait.
Do you see what I see?
What? What do you see?
I think that flower . . .
. . . is a *zinnia*!
Three Zs for *Zinnia*!

Oh! A *zinnia*. Perfect.
I'm done!
HELP!!!
Don't worry! We're all friendly here.
What now?

Do I have everything?
Check.
Check.
Check.

Ranger Anne? I think I have it all.

Nice job!
That rock is
beautiful!
I'm beautiful!
She said I'm
beautiful.
You're not
a rock.
I know.
But you're
still beautiful,
Stone.
Thank
you!

Great job, girls. Now let's say the Nature Girl motto.

Take nothing but pictures.
Leave nothing but footprints.
Keep nothing but memories.

Okay, back you go.
Goodbye!
Farewell!
See you again?
Roar!

Hey, where are we going?

Weren't you listening? We're going back home.
Home starts with H.
And *adventure* starts with A.
And you're a twig and he's a rock!
Tee-hee-hee.

And you're prickly!
Thank you!

See you around, Pinecone.
Not if I see you first.

Adventures are fun, but a little scary, too!

Some of the best things are!

Hey, Stick, I thought of a poem.

H is for *home*.
F is for *friend*.
And in this adventure,
E stands for . . .
The *End*!
That's beautiful, Stone.
Thank you.

The Nature Girl's A–Z Checklist

How many can YOU find?

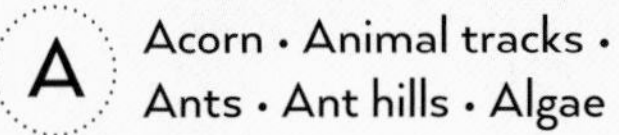

A Acorn • Animal tracks • Ants • Ant hills • Algae

B Beetle • Berries • Bees • Bark • Butterfly

C Clover • Creek bed • Cocoon • Caterpillar • Clouds • Cricket

D Dandelion • Dirt • Daffodil • Dogwood • Dragonfly • Dew

E Egg • Elm tree • Eagle • Egret • Erosion • Evergreen

F Fern • Feather • Frog • Fish • Fungus

G Grass • Grasshopper • Grain of sand • something Green

H Helicopter maple seed • Honeysuckle • Hive • Holly • Hummingbird

I Ivy • Inchworm • Iris • Insect

J Jewel weed • something Juicy • Jasmine • June bug • Jumping spider

K Kudzu • Katydid

L Leaf • Lily pad • Log • Ladybug • Lizard • Lightning bug • Lichen

M Moss • Mud • Mushroom • Mosquito • Moth

N Nest • Nut • Newt • Nettle • Nothing

O Oak leaf • Owl • something Oval • something Orange

P Pinecone • Pebble • Praying mantis • Pond skater • something Purple • Painted lady butterfly

Q Quail feather • Quartz

R Rock • Rose • Rabbit • something Red

S Snail • Stone • Stick • Seeds • Squirrel • Slug • Spider

T Twig • Tadpole • Tree • Toad • Turtle

U Unbroken branch • Underwing moth • Uniquely shaped leaf • Unusual rock • something Unexpected

V Vines • Vegetables • Violet • Valley • Viburnum

W Wildflower • Web • Worms • Weeds • Wasp • Wind • Wood • Wild Strawberry

X X-shaped twig

Y Yarrow • Yellowjacket • something Yellow • branch in the shape of a Y

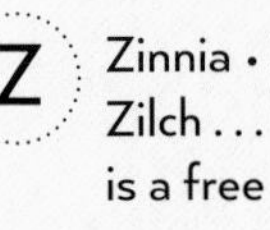

Z Zinnia • Zero • Zilch . . . This one is a free pass if you need it!

Stick and Stone and the Sticky Situation

Summer?

Close!

What's the best part of summer?

The beach?

Yes, but that's not it.

Fireflies?

Yes, but that's not it either.

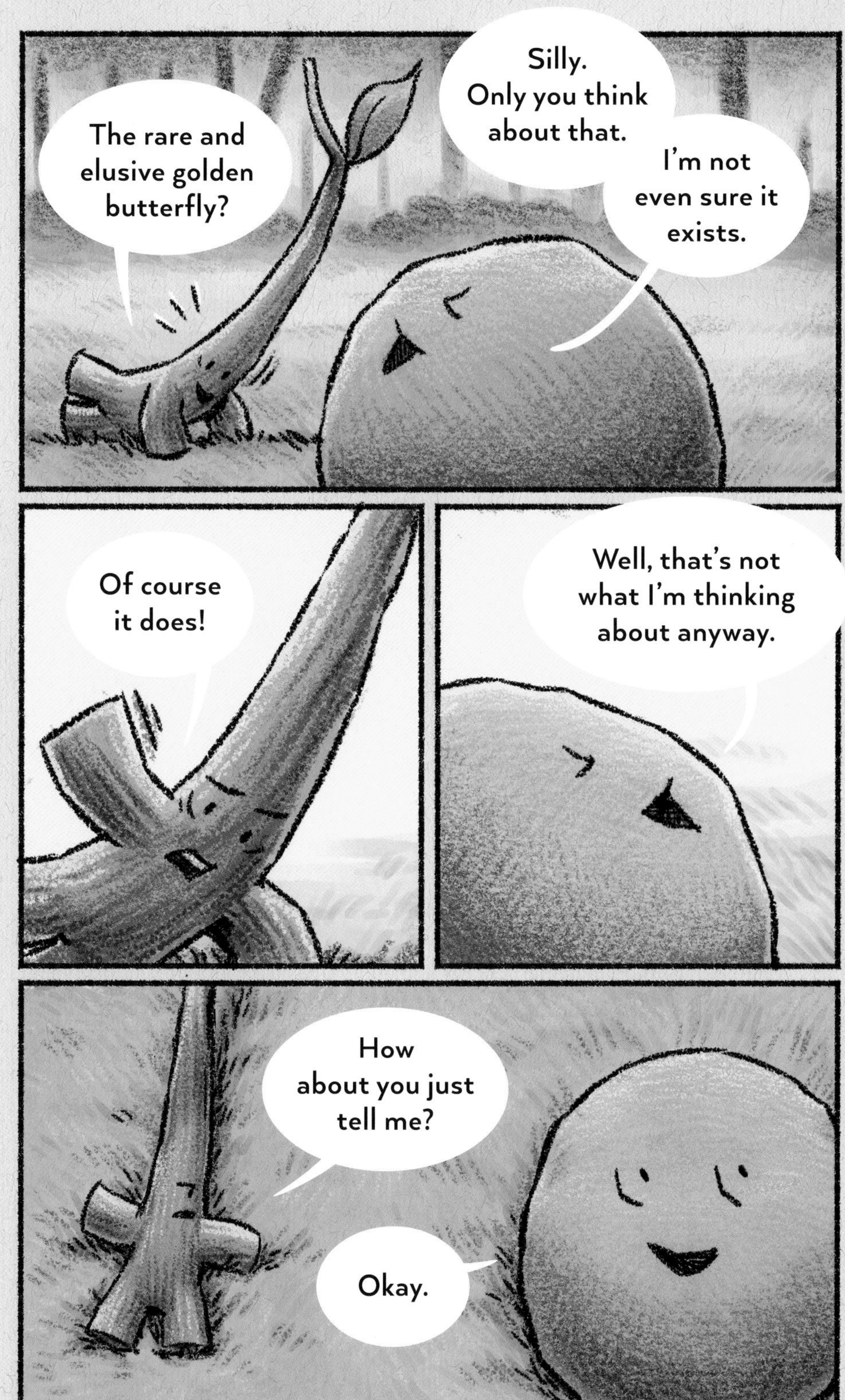
The rare and elusive golden butterfly?
Silly. Only you think about that.
I'm not even sure it exists.
Of course it does!
Well, that's not what I'm thinking about anyway.
How about you just tell me?
Okay.

I'm thinking about ice cream.
Oooh. Yum.
Now *I'm* thinking about ice cream.
Are you thinking about mint?
No.
Are you thinking about chocolate?
No.
Are you thinking . . . ?
How about I just tell you?
Okay.

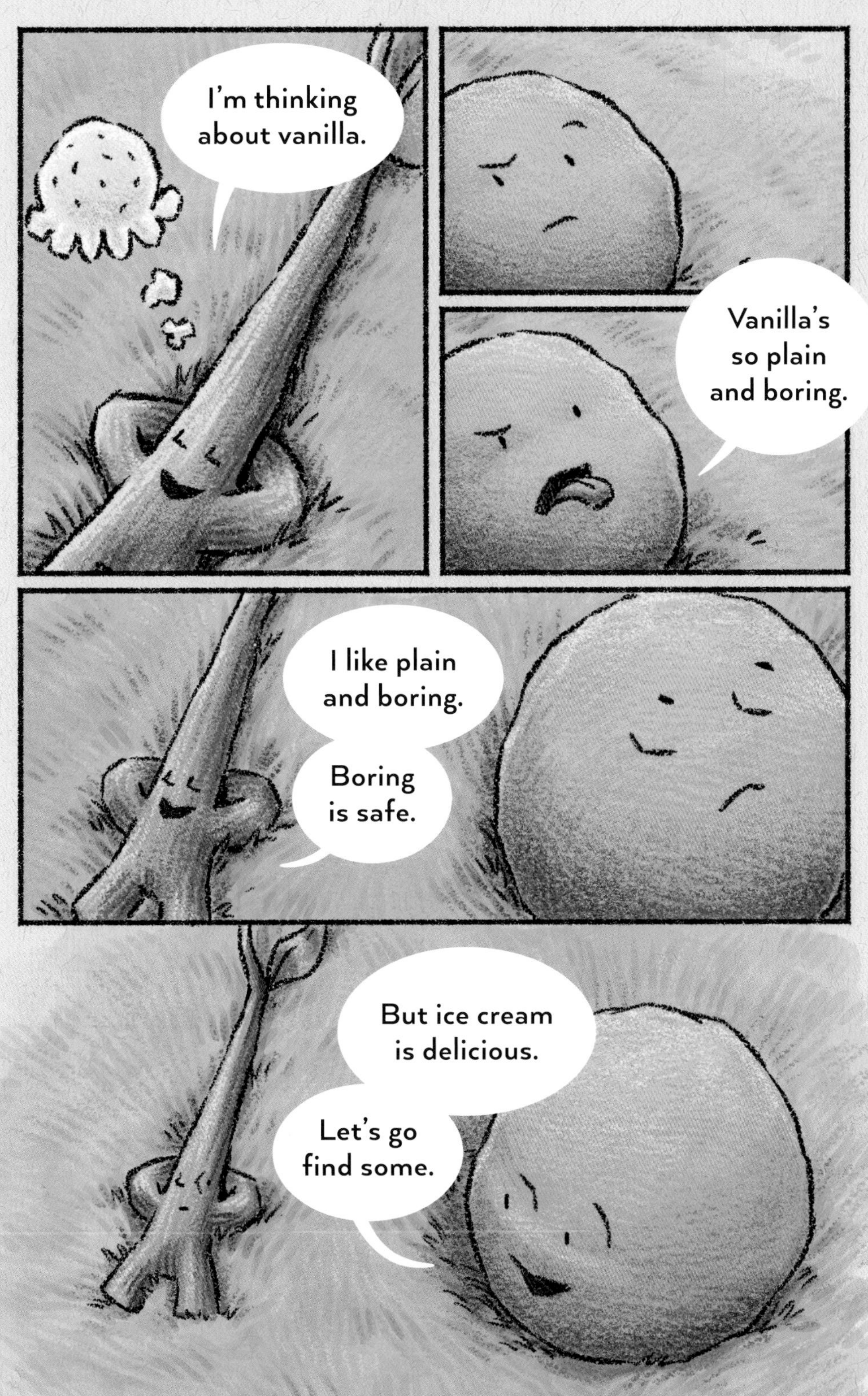
I'm thinking about vanilla.
Vanilla's so plain and boring.
I like plain and boring.
Boring is safe.
But ice cream is delicious.
Let's go find some.

I don't think there's any ice cream around here.
How about in the forest?

Maybe there's some in the FAR-est.

Where's the FAR-est?

Very far away from here.
Far, far away.

Let's go there.
Maybe the rare and elusive golden butterfly is there eating ice cream.

OR we could stay here and count my tomatoes.

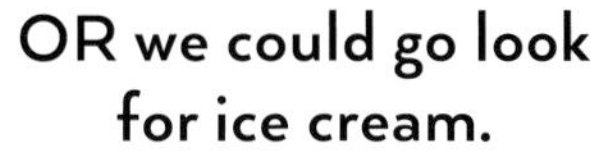
OR we could go look for ice cream.

Pretty please.

Okay.

How far do you think the FAR-est is?
I don't know.
Just far enough until we find ice cream.
Or see something interesting.

You know what's interesting?
Dandelions.
First they start off with yellow petals.
And then they turn into snowballs.
I wish they were real snowballs.
I've always wanted to eat some snow.
I wonder if snow tastes like ice cream.

I don't know, but I do know something cool.
Cool like ice cream?
No, cool like a fun fact.
What is it?
Once dandelions look like this, you can make a wish on them.
What?
Is that true?

Stick, are you joking with me?

I'd never joke about a wish.

Well, go ahead.
Go ahead and what?
Make a wish and blow on the dandelion.

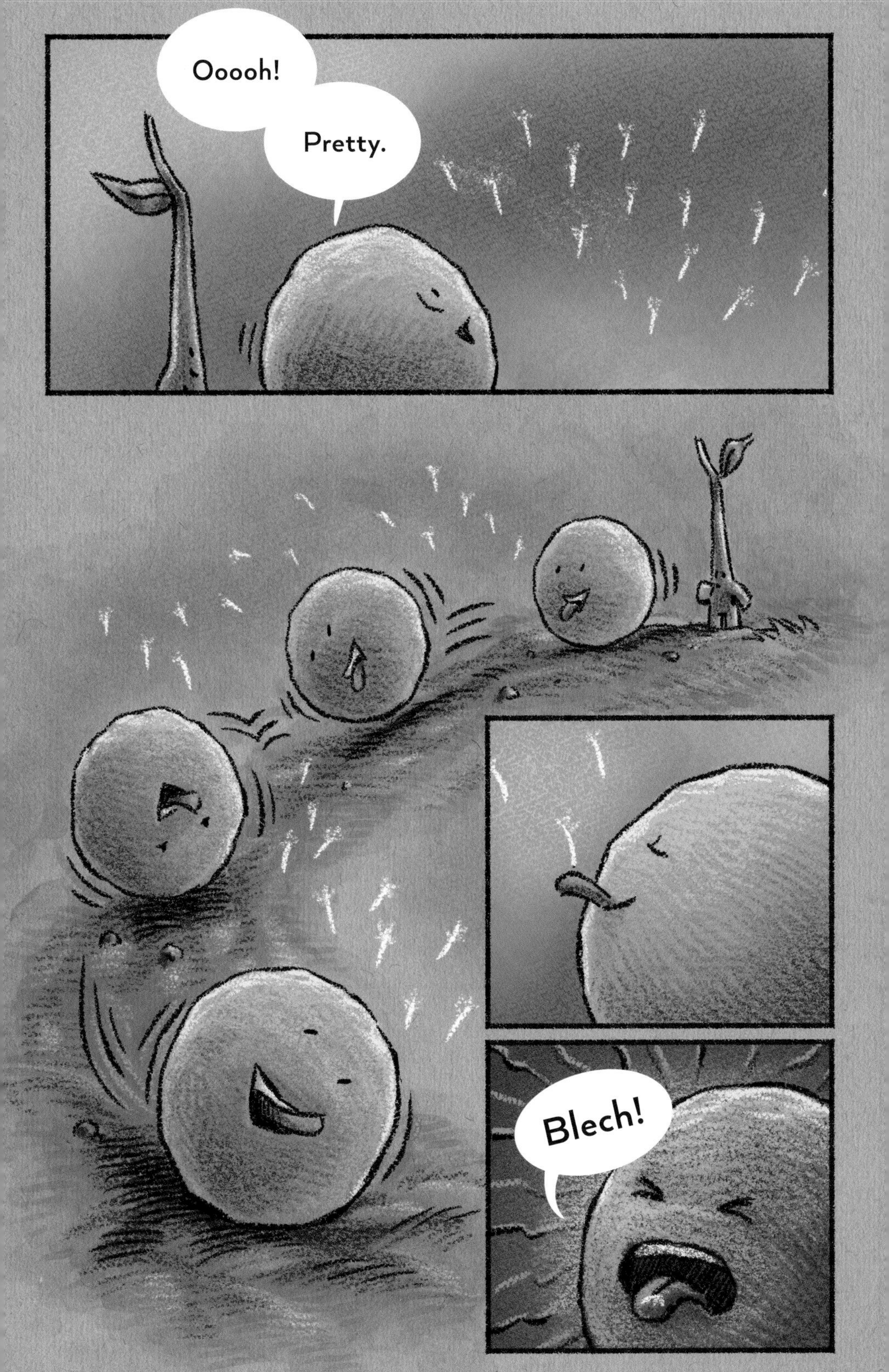

Ooooh!
Pretty.

Blech!

Well, I thought an adventure with snow might be better.

Didn't you get your fill of adventure with the Nature Girl?
You can never have too much adventure.
I'm not sure that's true.
I have definitely had enough adventure.
2
5
And I would be perfectly happy doing nothing but counting tomatoes and peas and fireflies.
6
4
1
3
Counting is boring.
CLIP!
CLOP!
CRUNCH!

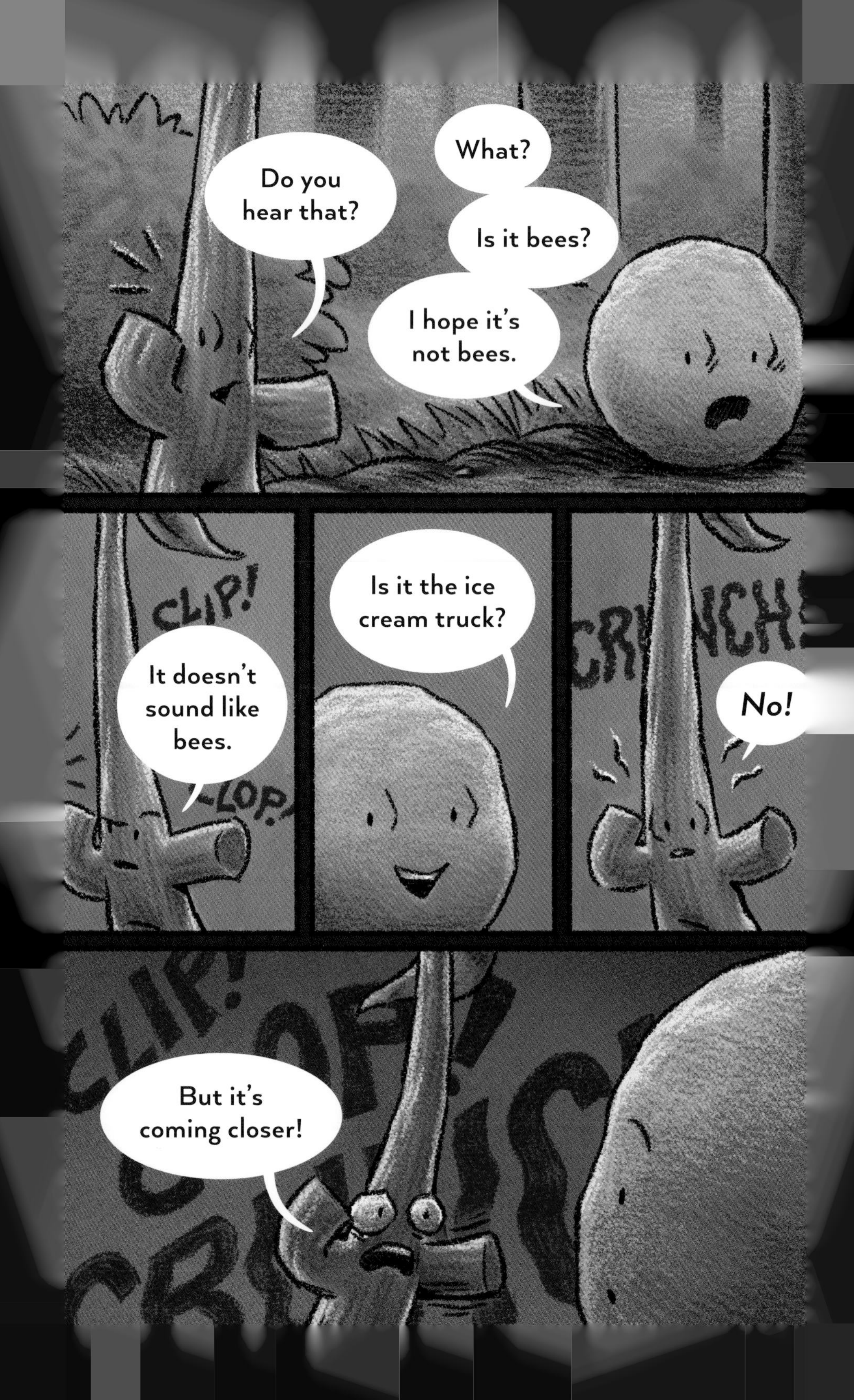
Do you hear that?
What?
Is it bees?
I hope it's not bees.
CLIP!
It doesn't sound like bees.
Is it the ice cream truck?
No!
CLIP!
But it's coming closer!

CLOP!
Feet!
Hands!
Oh no!
Not again!
CRUNCH!
Adventure, here we come!

Wait up!

I'm
coming
too!

I'm sure it
will be fine!
This will
be fine!
We will
be fine!

I hope this adventure involves snow.
I hope this adventure doesn't last very long.
Those fireflies are just waiting to be counted.
Oh, look . . .
. . . it's the beach.

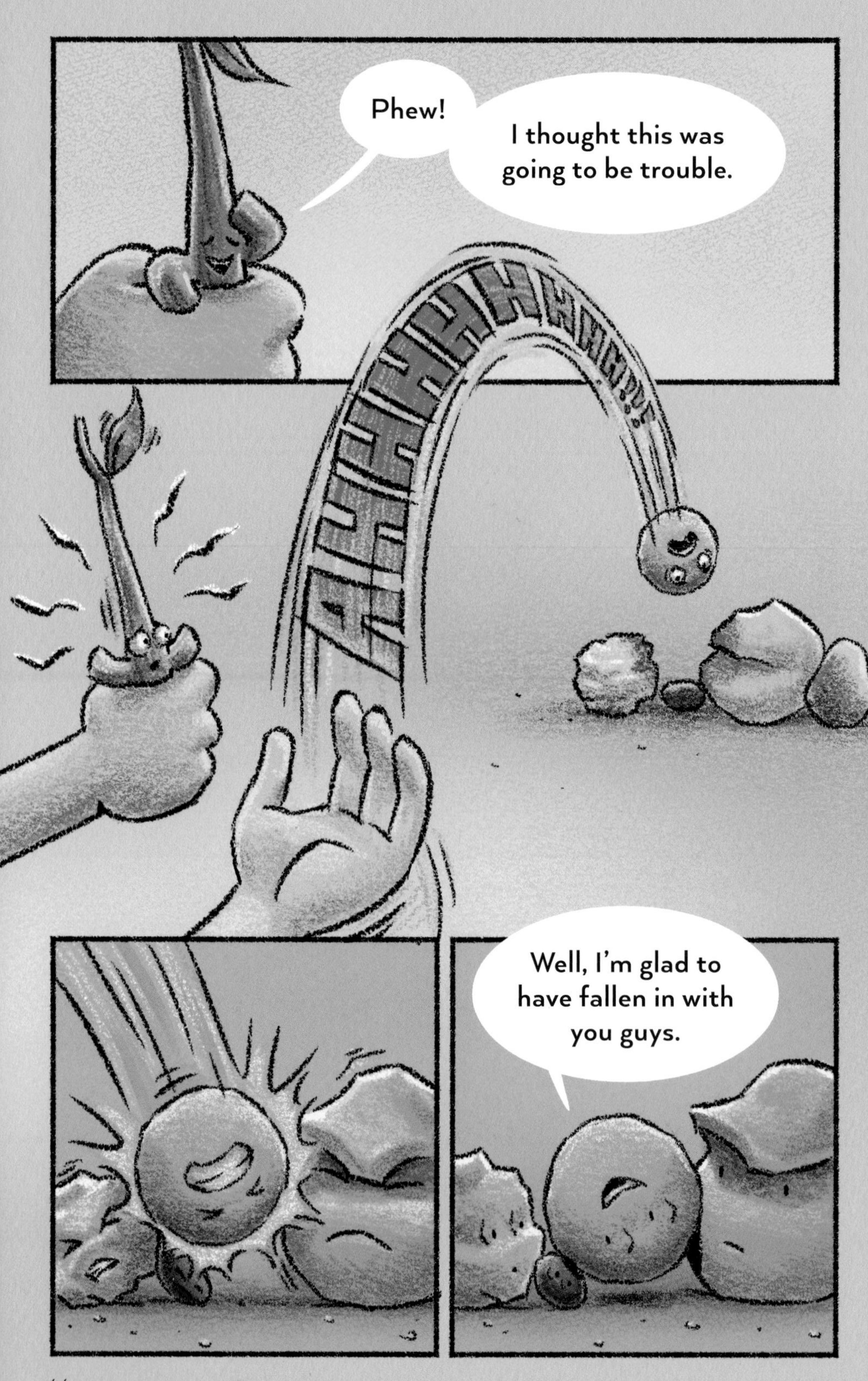
Phew!
I thought this was going to be trouble.
AHHHHHHHHHH!!!
Well, I'm glad to have fallen in with you guys.

Hello,
I'm Rock!
Hi, I'm
Pebble.
I'm Stone.
I'm Boulder.

You don't look
big enough to be
a boulder.
Wanna piece of me?

No, thank
you. You look
like a very
nice, smallish
boulder.
Thank you!

I'm Stone too.

Can I call you
Stone Two?
Sure!

It's nice to meet all of you.
What a great day!
What are you so happy about?
What are you so grumpy about?
We've been sitting here in this pile all day.
Maybe they're going to build a castle with us.
I've always wanted to be part of a sandcastle.
I'm pretty sure they're going to throw us in the ocean.

Me neither.

We'll all sink!

Sink.

Sank.

Sunk.

I guess they're not going
to throw us in the ocean.

I knew it!
I knew we'd be okay.
And just look at the pretty red flower.
That's not a flower.

I'm feeling a little warm.

Warm? I feel positively HOT.

This flower has some heating power.

It's not a flower.
It's fire.

And fire can get so hot it can melt stones.

Gasp!
Gulp!

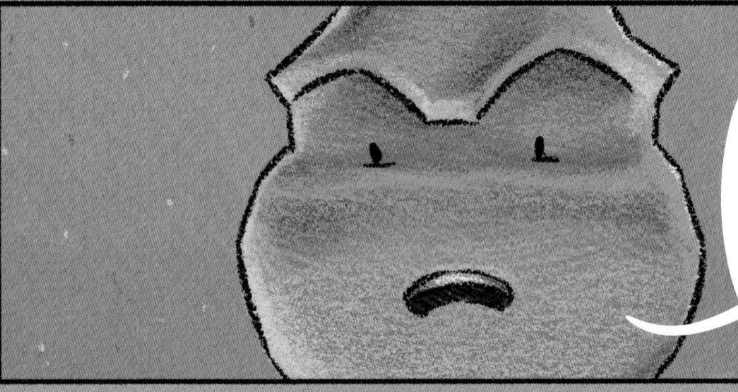
And we'd all turn into lava and we'd have to live in a volcano.

A volcano sounds *so* familiar.
I think I may have been born in a volcano.
Cool!
It was definitely not cool.

Well, unless something happens quick, we are all going to be hot potatoes!

I don't want
to be a potato.
I am perfectly
happy being a stone.
And where's
Stick, anyway?
Who's
Stick?
My best
friend.
Is he
tall?
Yup.
Is he
brown?
Yup.
Does he have
white hair?
No. What?

Stick?
Is that you?
Stone?
I'm in trouble up here.
We're in trouble too.
Wait . . . what's on your head?
They call it a marshmallow.
That looks a bit tricky.
It's actually very sticky.
Why did they put a marshmallow on your head?
I heard something about toasting.

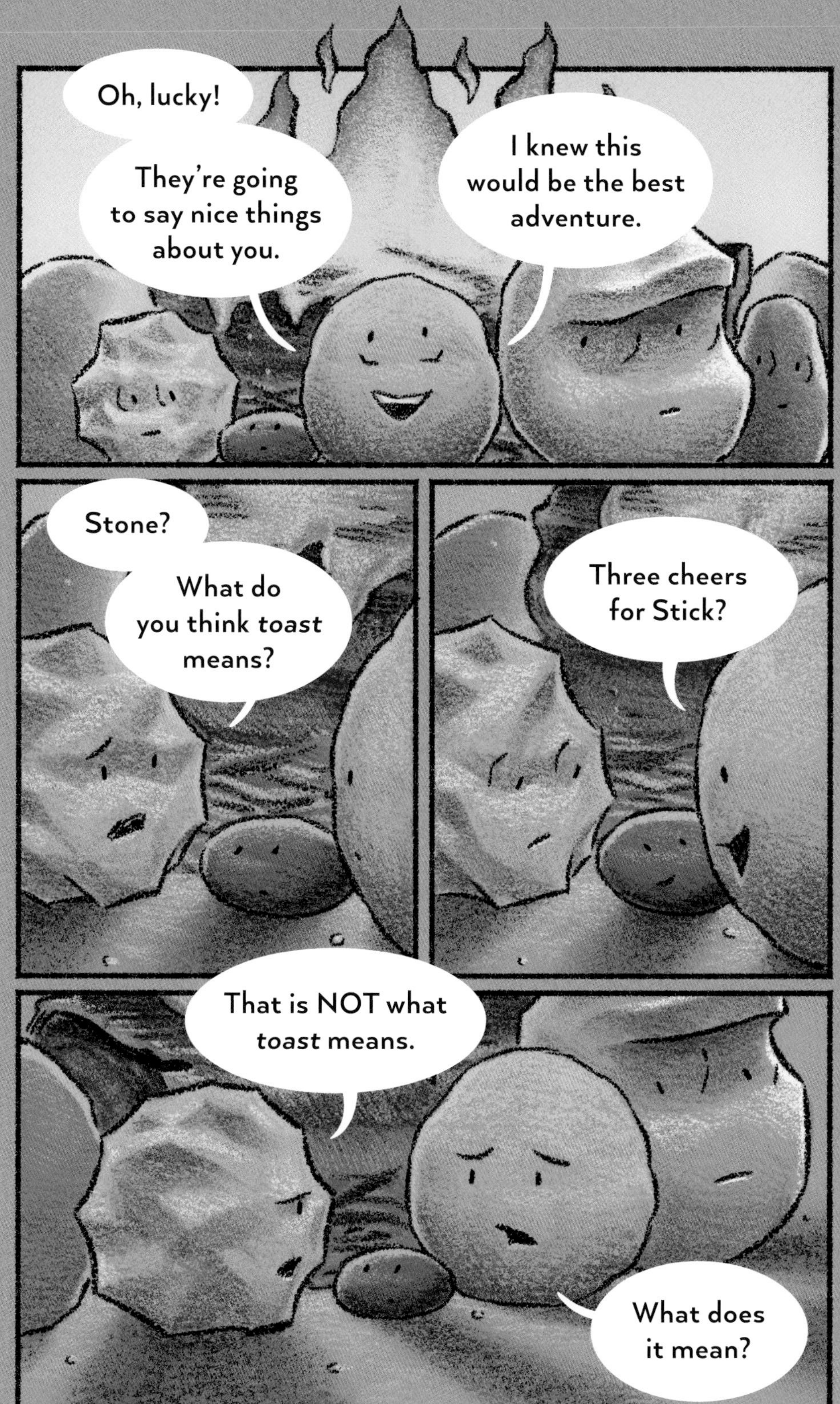
Oh, lucky!
They're going to say nice things about you.
I knew this would be the best adventure.
Stone?
What do you think *toast* means?
Three cheers for Stick?
That is NOT what *toast* means.
What does it mean?

It means getting cooked over a fire.
This fire, I would guess.
GASP!
GULP
AAAHHHH!!!
I knew adventures were bad.
Bad adventure!

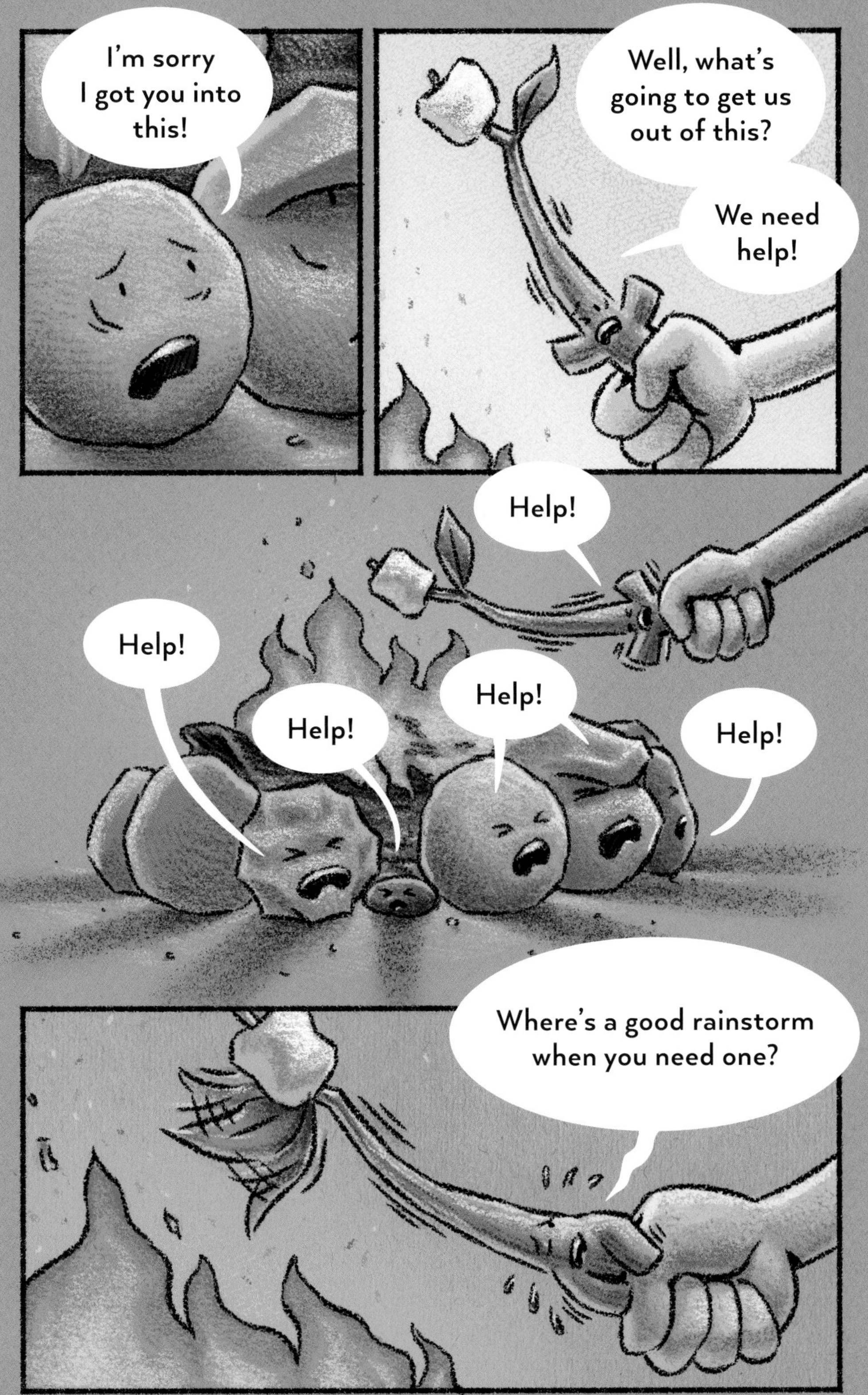

I'm sorry
I got you into
this!
Well, what's
going to get us
out of this?
We need
help!
Help!
Help!
Help!
Help!
Help!
Where's a good rainstorm
when you need one?

BOOOOM
Did you just do that?
I don't *think* so.
You asked for a rainstorm and now there's thunder?
Maybe you're not a stick.
Maybe you're a magic wand.
Maybe I am. Let me try a magic spell.

Rain. Rain.
Come today.
Make
this fire go
away.
All hail
Stick!
Maybe you're
magic too, Stone!
Maybe
I am.

Three cheers for Stick!
Three cheers for Stone!

See you later,
craters.

I got
kicked.
I got
flicked.

My butt
got roasted.

I almost got
toasted. And look
at my head.

I must admit,
you've looked
better.

But I've never felt better.
I made it rain.
You sure did!
But, Stick?
Yes?
I think I'm done with adventures.
Really?
Yup!
I'm not very good at counting, but I'd be happy to count tomatoes with you.

You might not be good at counting, but I can always count on you!
Thanks for not leaving me.

I'd never leave you!
Now let's go home!

That's the best idea I've ever heard.
But first . . .

Where are you going?
To take a bath!

Hey, Stone—look!

It's a starfish!
Should we make a new wish?
Absolutely!

I wish . . .

Think it. Don't say it.

What did you wish for?
You just told me not to say it.
I know, but I'm your best friend and I think it's okay to share your wish with your best friend.
I wished for ice cream.
Ice cream?
Ice cream?

We are on a beach far from home, where we almost got toasted and roasted, and you wished for ice cream?

Well, if I had wished for ice cream in the first place, instead of adventure, we wouldn't be in this mess.

I wished to be bigger.
Like a branch?
No, like a giant redwood tree.
No one would put a marshmallow on a tree!

Or on a mountain.
I should have wished to be a mountain.
Covered with lots and lots of snow!
How about tiny?

If you could be tiny, what would you be?
I'd be a grain of sand so I could laze on the beach all day.
I'd be a tiny bonsai tree.
How about dazzling?
If you could be dazzling, what would you be?

I know!
I know!
I'd be a sparkler.
I'd dazzle and sizzle and send out golden sparks!
You would make the best sparkler!
I'd be a geode.
All brown and lumpy on the outside, but dazzling on the inside.
Wow!

If you could go anywhere, where would you go?
I'd go to the Amazon and see all the rainforests.
I'd meet frogs and birds and butterflies.
Lots of butterflies.
Maybe even . . .
. . . the rare and elusive golden butterfly.
You wouldn't go without me, Stick, would you?

Of course not.
We'd go to all these places together.
Well then, I think I'd go to the desert where the red rocks glow.
I'd love to see the red rocks.
Okay, last question, Stone.

If you could be anything, what would you wish to be?
Stick, as long as you're you, I'd wish to be me!
That sounds like the best wish I've ever heard.
You're the best friend I've ever had!
Thanks, Stone.
Let's go home.

S'mores Recipe

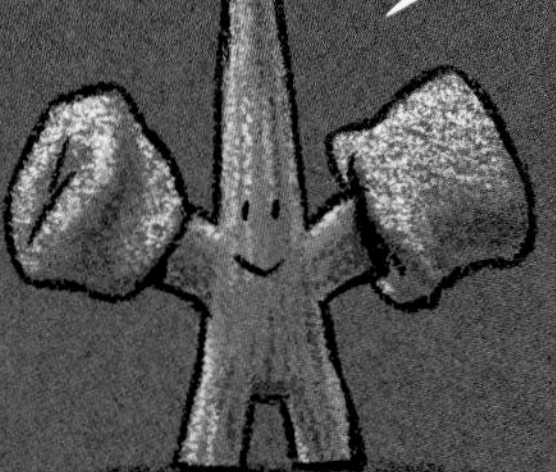

Ingredients:

Marshmallows
Chocolate bars
Graham crackers

Traditional campfire method

- Place a marshmallow on the stick and toast till ooey-gooey.
- Slide marshmallow off the stick and onto a graham cracker square.
- Place a square of chocolate over the marshmallow.
- Top with a second graham cracker square and SMOOSH them together.
- Take a bite and then have s'more!

Oven method (makes many)

- Preheat oven to 350 degrees.
- Line a baking sheet with parchment paper.
- Lay graham cracker squares on paper, then top with a square of chocolate and a marshmallow.
- Bake 4–6 minutes, until marshmallow is puffy and chocolate is soft.
- Remove from oven and top with another graham cracker square and SMOOSH!

Microwave method (makes one)

- Place two graham cracker squares on a microwave-safe plate.
- Place a chocolate square on one cracker and a marshmallow on the other.
- Microwave for 15–20 seconds.
- Remove from microwave and flip one cracker on top of the other, then SMOOSH!

For Kate, who started this adventure and made every minute of it fun! —B.F.
To Mom for the encouragement, Tom for the opportunities, and both for their steadfast support. —K.C.

Clarion Books is an imprint of HarperCollins Publishers. · HarperAlley is an imprint of HarperCollins Publishers. Stick and Stone Explore and More · Manufactured in Bosnia and Herzegovina. For information address HarperCollins Children's Books, a division of HarperCollins Publishers, 195 Broadway, New York, NY 10007. · www.harperalley.com · ISBN 978-0-35-854936-9 — ISBN 978-0-35-854934-5 (pbk.) · The artist created the digital illustrations for this book with a drawing tablet, using brushes simulating pencils and watercolors and scans of drawing paper. · Typography by Alice Wang and Michelle Cunningham · 23 24 25 26 27 GPS 10 9 8 7 6 5 4 3 2 1 · First paperback edition, 2023

s the author of several picture
:k and Stone* and *Stick and Stone: Best Friends Forever!* She lives in New Jersey.

KRISTEN CELLA has been drawing since she could hold a pencil, though these days she usually uses a digital stylus. She lives in Chicago.

Also available as an ebook.

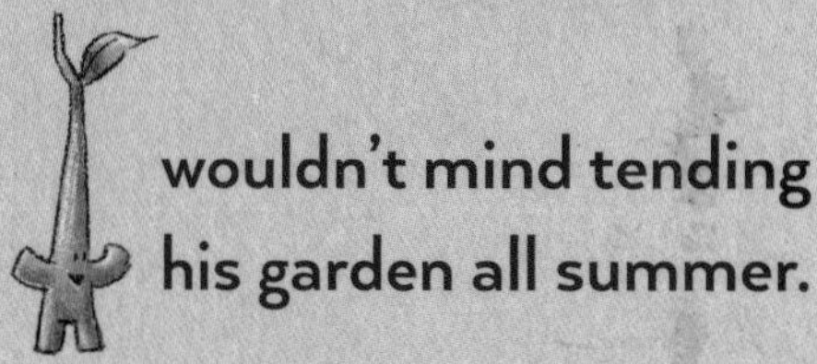

wouldn't mind tending his garden all summer.

has been itching for something more.

From A to Z, from the forest to the beach, Stick and Stone discover that everything is *s'more* fun when they explore together.

Join Stick and Stone as they get swept up in a scavenger hunt. Accompany them to a campfire calamity. And laugh along with them in this new graphic novel series starring two best buddies and a whole cast of new characters. Each story has a fun activity to make you feel like you're part of the action.

But don't just *stick* to these two stories—there's more!

Clarion Books
Imprints of HarperCollinsPublishers

HARPER alley

Ages 6–10

Cover design by Whitney Leader-Picone

harperalley.com

US $7.99 / $9.99 CAN

ISBN 978-0-35-854934-5

9 780358 549345 50799

0123

Wampum Belts of the Iroquois

Tehanetorens